Published in the United States of America by Star Bright Books, Inc., New York. The name Star Bright Books and the Star Bright Books logo are registered trademarks of Star Bright Books, Inc. Please visit www.starbrightbooks.com.

ISBN-13:  978-1-932065-98-5
ISBN-10:  1-932065-98-9

Printed in China  9 8 7 6 5 4 3 2 1

Library of Congress Cataloging-in-Publication Data

Huggins, Peter.
  Trosclair and the alligator / by Peter Huggins ; illustrated by Lindsey Gardiner.
      p. cm.
  Summary: Trosclair ignores his father's warning about Gargantua, the rogue alligator living in nearby Bayou Fontaine, and heads off into Bee Island Swamp to hunt for turtle eggs.
  ISBN-13: 978-1-932065-98-5
  ISBN-10: 1-932065-98-9
  [1. Alligators--Fiction. 2. Swamps--Fiction. 3. Louisiana--Fiction.]  I. Gardiner, Lindsey, ill.
II. Title.

PZ7.H87307Tro 2005
[E]--dc22
                                                                                2005017296

# Trosclair and the Alligator

By Peter Huggins   Illustrated by Lindsey Gardiner

Star Bright Books
New York

Trosclair loved living on Bayou Fontaine in Louisiana.

He could hop into his pirogue anytime and hunt turtles or visit his cousins.

And while Trosclair played
cards with his cousins, Aunt Emilie
and Uncle Maurice fixed gumbo
and rice in the kitchen.

Whenever he visited, Uncle Maurice
would say, "Trosclair, how you been keeping, you?"

Trosclair would say, "Me, I been keeping fine."
Then they would laugh.

When Trosclair didn't go
to his cousins, he and his
dog, Ollie, would glide in the
pirogue to Bee Island Swamp,
the best place to hunt turtle eggs.

Trosclair wasn't supposed to go to the swamp
because Gargantua, the rogue alligator, had moved in.
He scared everyone. He attacked dogs, cats, goats,
and a few careless pigs.

Père, Trosclair's father, said it was only a matter
of time before Gargantua tried boy or man.

"That alligator eat you and Ollie so fast,"
Père said, "he won't even
stop to burp."

Trosclair wasn't so sure.
Besides, he loved the swamp.
Gliding under the cypress
trees on the smooth water,
Trosclair listened to the
silence, broken by the
dip, dip, dip of his paddle,
or the cry of a heron.

Trosclair beached his pirogue on
    Bee Island at the center of the swamp.
        He didn't see or hear Gargantua once.

Trosclair and Ollie hunted turtle eggs but didn't find any. They did find a bee hive in a live oak tree. Trosclair thought the honey would taste *really* good.

Trosclair picked up a stick. He and Ollie stepped onto a log at the foot of the tree. They stepped onto a low-hanging branch.

Then onto a higher branch. . .

. . .and then an even higher branch.
Trosclair helped Ollie onto the
last branch as the bees
buzzed all around
them.

Below them,
the log moved.

The log was GARGANTUA!

After Gargantua unwrapped himself
from around the tree, Trosclair saw he
was as long as Père and Uncle Maurice
laid head-to-toe, head-to-toe.

Trosclair looked at Ollie and
Ollie looked at Trosclair.

Then Ollie barked at Gargantua.

Gargantua looked up at them and grinned.
They could see how many teeth he had.
And how big they were!


"Well, well, my petits are stuck in a tree," said Gargantua.
"I tell you what you do, boy.
You trow dat dog down to me,
and I leave you alone, eh?"

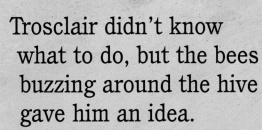

Trosclair didn't know
what to do, but the bees
buzzing around the hive
gave him an idea.

He winked at Ollie. Trosclair said,
"Okay, Gargantua, open your mouth,
and I'll drop Ollie right in.

"I sure am glad you don't
want the beehive."

Gargantua looked

first at Ollie,

then at the beehive,

and back at Ollie.

"Come closer," said Trosclair.

Gargantua didn't move.
The bees buzzed around
Trosclair and Ollie.

"What's a beehive?"
asked Gargantua.

"Oh," said Trosclair, waving the bees away.

"It's just full to bursting of the sweetest, TASTIEST honey you've ever seen. I'm glad you don't want it!"

"Sweet, huh?" said Gargantua. Gargantua thought a minute as the bees buzzed around the hive. "I tell you what you do," Gargantua said. "You trow dat old beehive down to me, and I let you keep dat dog."

"NOT THAT!" said Trosclair.
"Anything but that."

"Please take my dog and let me keep the beehive."
"NO!" said Gargantua.
"PLEASE, PLEASE take my dog," Trosclair begged.

"No, my mind, she is made up!"
Gargantua said.

"Well, all right," Trosclair said.
"Only, you have to come closer!"

Gargantua moved the
length of his knobby,
swamp-colored body closer.

When Gargantua was directly under the beehive, Trosclair yelled, "STOP!"

"Now open your mouth!" Trosclair said.

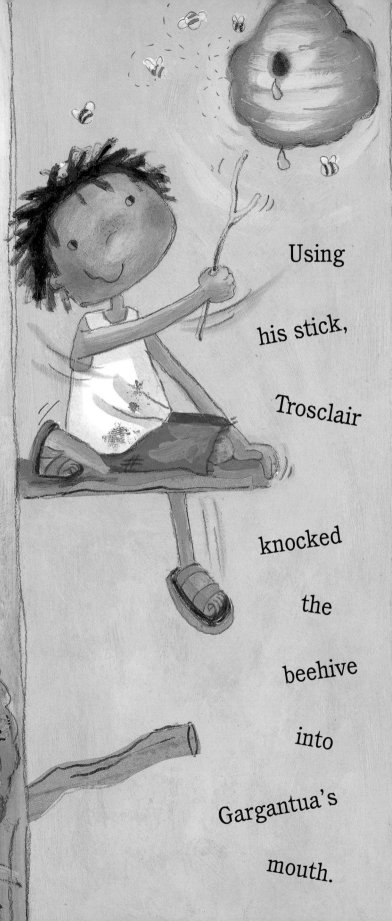

Using his stick, Trosclair knocked the beehive into Gargantua's mouth.

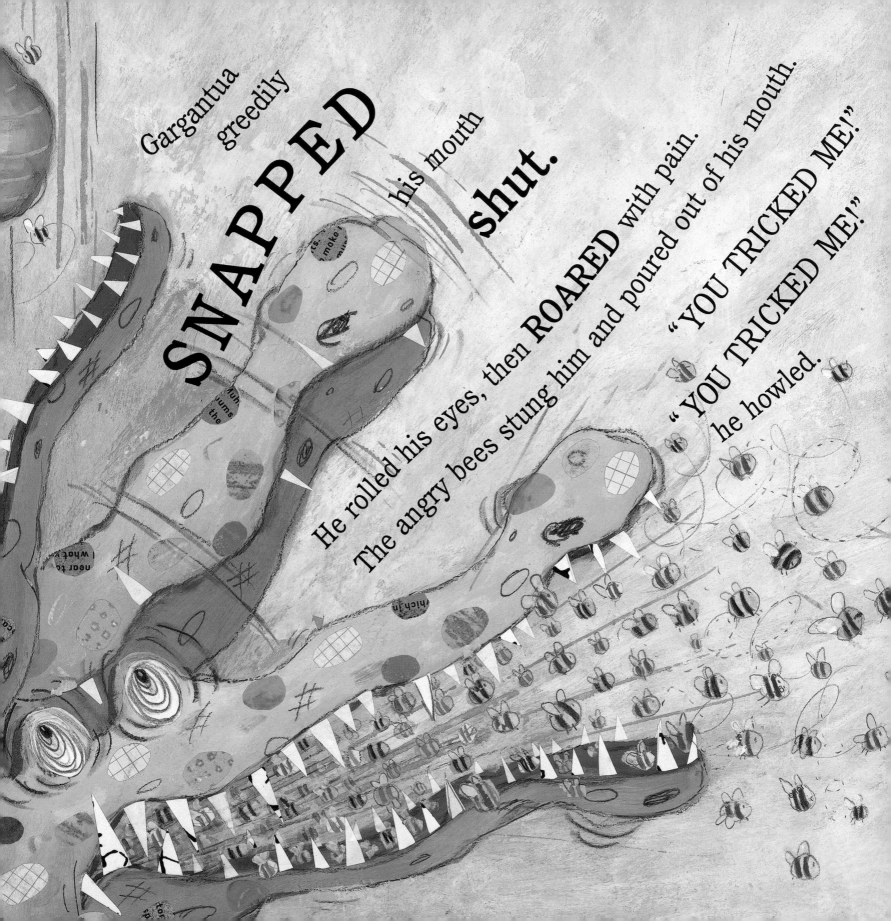

Gargantua greedily SNAPPED his mouth shut.

He rolled his eyes, then ROARED with pain.

The angry bees stung him and poured out of his mouth.

"YOU TRICKED ME!"

"YOU TRICKED ME!" he howled.

Gargantua ran as fast as he could to the water, pursued by the swarming bees. . . .

. . . and he didn't stop swimming until
Bee Island Swamp was far
behind him.

When Trosclair and Ollie got back home, Père said,
"Where you been now? Your Uncle Maurice said he
saw that Gargantua heading down da bayou like the
swamp wolf were after it."

"Père, that old alligator got him a sweet tooth.
He'll never come back here."

"I guess the animals be safe now.
An' safe for you to go back to the swamp.
What you say?" asked Père.

"I'll go tomorrow, Père,"
Trosclair said.

But for a long time, Trosclair never went
to Bee Island Swamp without Père or
Uncle Maurice or one of his cousins.

And to this day,
Gargantua has never come back.